Based on the episode "Catboy and the Great Birthday Cake Rescue"

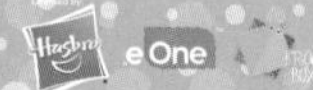

SIMON SPOTLIGHT
An imprint of Simon & Schuster Children's Publishing Division • New York London Toronto Sydney New Delhi • 1230 Avenue of the Americas, New York, New York 10020
This Simon Spotlight paperback edition June 2021 • Adapted by Tina Gallo from the series PJ Masks

For information about special discounts for bulk purchases, please contact Simon & Schuster Special Sales at 1-866-506-1949 or business@simonandschuster.com.
Manufactured in the United States of America 0521 LAK • 2 4 6 8 10 9 7 5 3 1 • ISBN 978-1-5344-7000-2 (pbk) • ISBN 978-1-5344-7001-9 (ebook)

Greg is excited about his lizard-themed birthday party! It is happening today at lunchtime, and the party room is already decorated with green balloons and banners with lizards on them. All the food will be green, too!

He's even going to have a special green lizard cake . . . but when he brings Amaya and Connor to see it, the cake is gone!

Greg sees purple Ninjalino footprints all over the floor of the room. "That means Night Ninja has my cake!" he cries.

The trio agrees that this is a job for the PJ Masks.

PJ MASKS, WE'RE ON OUR WAY! INTO THE NiGHT TO SAVE THE DAY!

Greg becomes Gekko!

Connor becomes Catboy!
Amaya becomes Owlette!
They are the PJ Masks!

The PJ Masks jump into the Gekko-Mobile.
"Let's go get my lizard cake!" Gekko cheers.

Suddenly, Gekko brings the Gekko-Mobile to a screeching halt.
"Gasping Gekkos!" he cries.
Two Ninjalinos are carrying his lizard cake!

Owlette, Gekko, and Catboy race after the Ninjalinos, only to be stopped and greeted by Night Ninja.

"It's the PJ Masks!" he shouts. "Are you coming to admire my cake?"

"That's *my* lizard cake!" Gekko says.

"Not anymore," Night Ninja tells him. "It's *my* cake now and *my* party! Ha ha ha!"

All the Ninjalinos cheer!

Catboy challenges Night Ninja to a party game to distract him.

"Fine," Night Ninja says. "We'll play musical chairs. And the winner gets—"

Catboy gasps. The prize is a bunch of Master Fang balloons! Master Fang is Catboy's favorite!

Gekko tells Catboy to delay the game to give Gekko and Owlette time to grab the cake. Catboy is so excited about the balloons that he forgets all about the plan and Gekko's lizard cake.

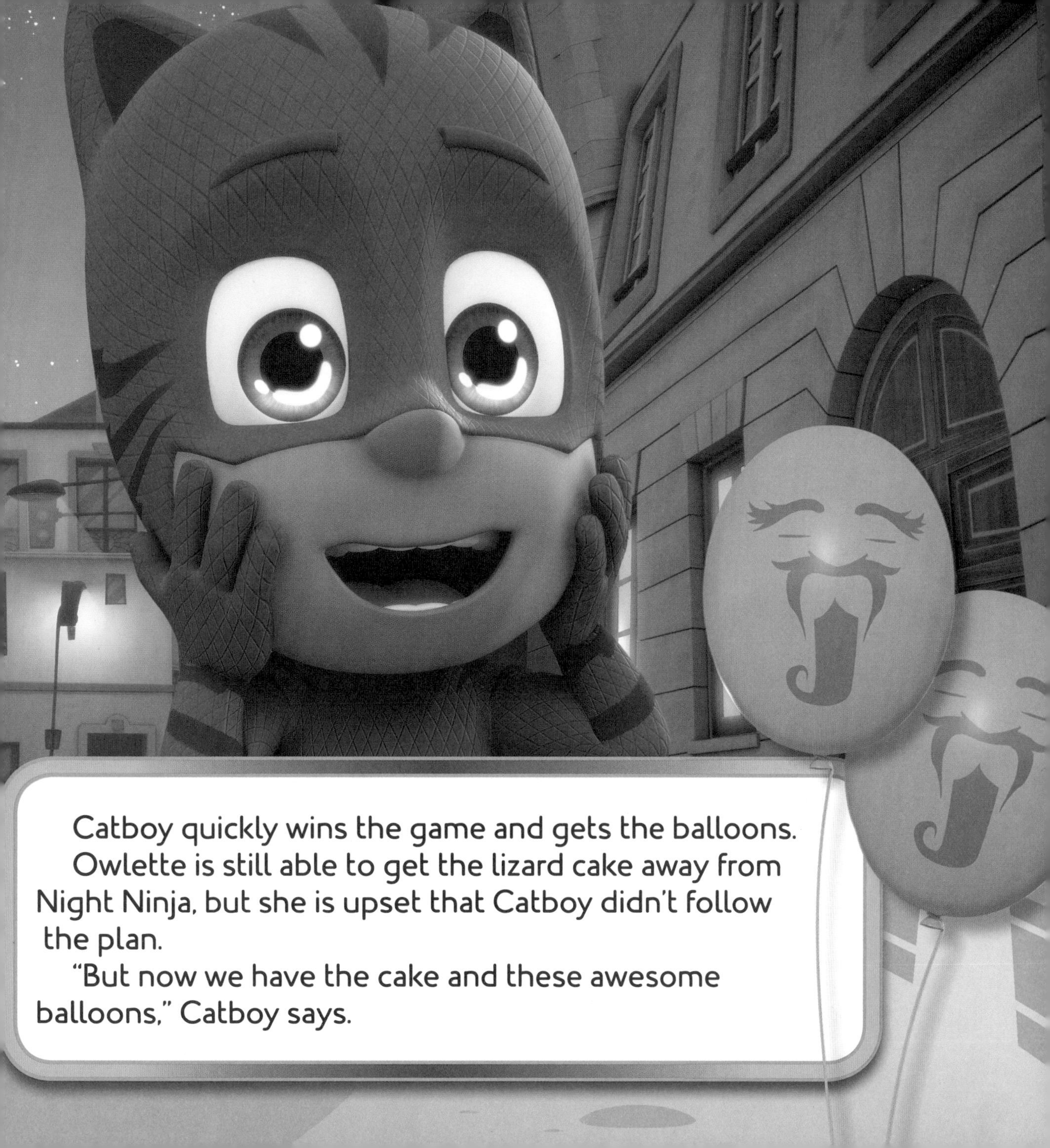

Catboy quickly wins the game and gets the balloons.
Owlette is still able to get the lizard cake away from Night Ninja, but she is upset that Catboy didn't follow the plan.
"But now we have the cake and these awesome balloons," Catboy says.

Suddenly, Night Ninja is back with a Master Fang birthday cake.

He offers to swap it for the lizard cake.

Before Gekko can say anything, Catboy makes the swap! He really likes Master Fang.

Night Ninja tells the PJ Masks the Master Fang cake is actually a Sticky Splat Whipped Cream Splato cake!

When all the layers light up, the cake will splatter whipped cream everywhere.

When people try to clean up the whipped cream, they'll all get stuck because of the Sticky Splat!

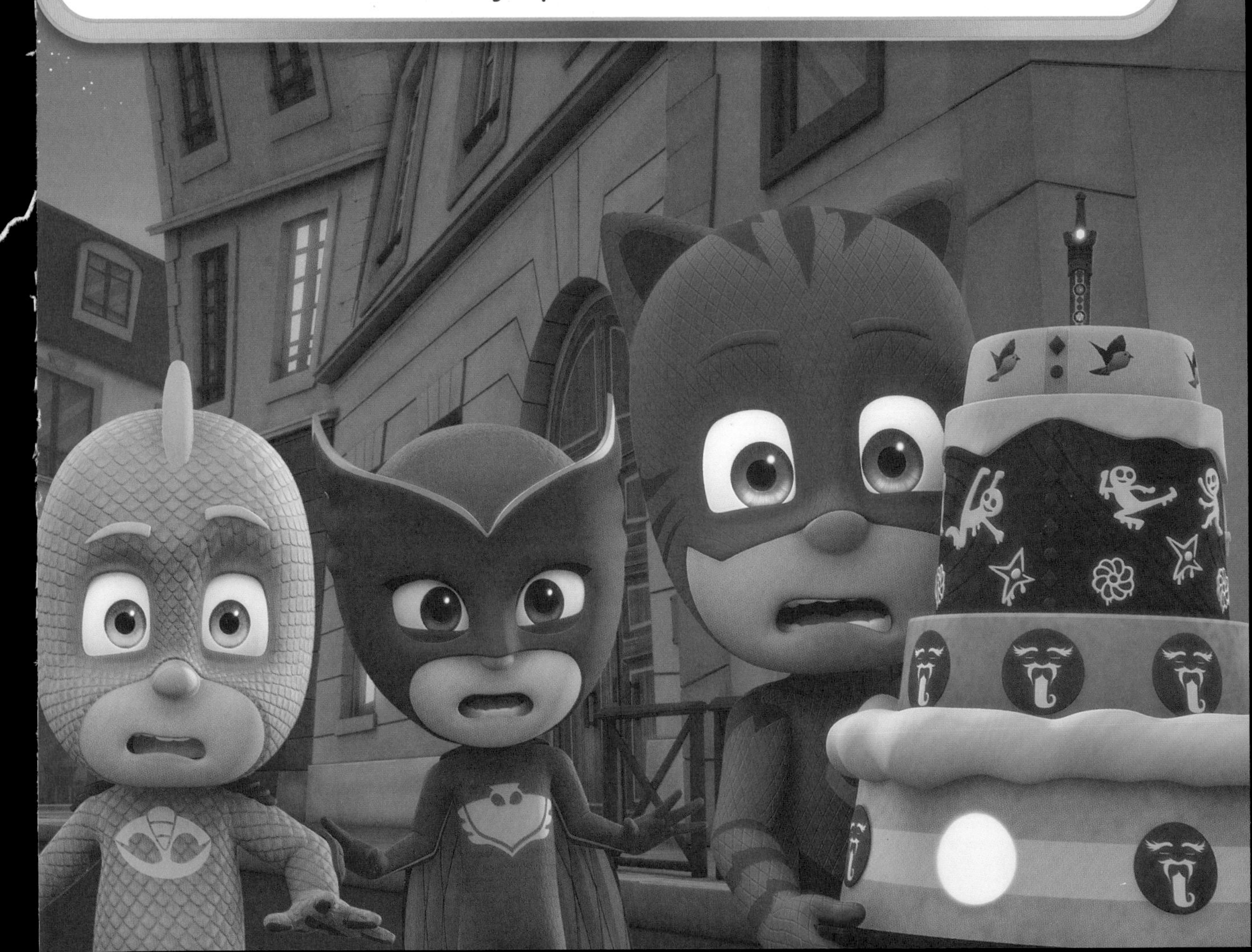

Catboy feels terrible. "I'm sorry, Gekko. This is all my fault, but I have an idea. It's time to be a hero!"

Catboy, Owlette, and Gekko pretend to be playing a fun game. The first one in the Gekko-Mobile when the music stops wins!

Night Ninja hears the commotion and hops into the Gekko-Mobile.

"I win!" he shouts. Then he notices the Master Fang cake behind him.

The cake splatters sticky whipped cream all over Night Ninja! While the Ninjalinos laugh, Catboy takes back the lizard cake!

PJ Masks all shout hooray!
'Cause in the night we saved the day!
"And Gekko's cake!" says Catboy.